This book belongs
to Mayah Salih

Puss in Boots

and other fairytales

Puss in Boots

and other fairytales

Retold by Stephanie Laslett

‖ · PARRAGON · ‖

A PARRAGON BOOK

Published by
Parragon Publishing,
Queen Street House, 4 Queen Street,
Bath BA1 1HE

Produced by
The Templar Company plc,
Pippbrook Mill, London Road, Dorking,
Surrey RH4 1JE

Printed and bound in China.
ISBN 0 75253 121 2

Contents

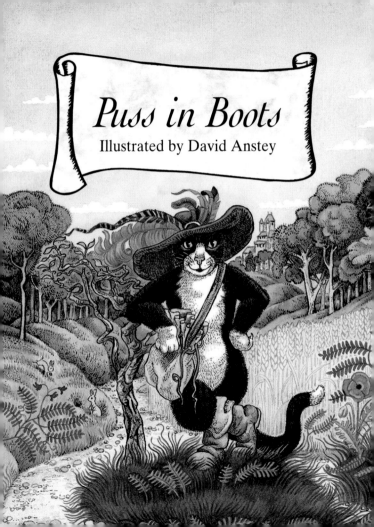

Puss in Boots

Illustrated by David Anstey

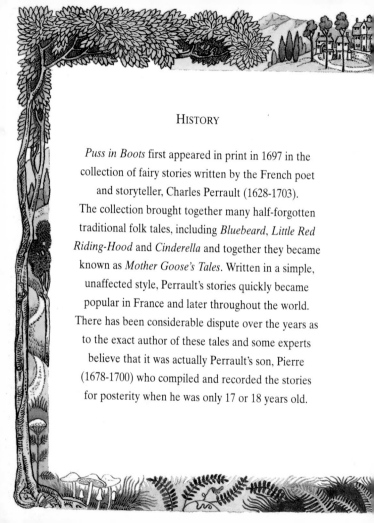

History

Puss in Boots first appeared in print in 1697 in the
collection of fairy stories written by the French poet
and storyteller, Charles Perrault (1628-1703).
The collection brought together many half-forgotten
traditional folk tales, including *Bluebeard*, *Little Red
Riding-Hood* and *Cinderella* and together they became
known as *Mother Goose's Tales*. Written in a simple,
unaffected style, Perrault's stories quickly became
popular in France and later throughout the world.
There has been considerable dispute over the years as
to the exact author of these tales and some experts
believe that it was actually Perrault's son, Pierre
(1678-1700) who compiled and recorded the stories
for posterity when he was only 17 or 18 years old.

There was once an old miller who had three sons. After some time, the miller fell ill and when he knew he was about to die, he called in his sons and divided his property between them. He did not own much and so the deed was soon done. To his eldest son he gave his mill, to his second son he gave his donkey and to his youngest son he gave his cat.

Now the youngest son
was very unhappy to be
left such a small share
of his father's belongings.

"You two can join together with your mill and your donkey and you will always have plenty of work," he complained to his brothers. "But what am I to do? Having a cat will not help me to earn

money. All he is good
for is catching mice.
Now I will surely starve
to death!"

Now the cat heard all
this, and spoke to the
youngest son in a grave
and serious voice.

"Do not worry, my good master. All you have to do is give me a bag, and get a pair of boots made for me, so I may scamper through the dirt and the brambles, and you will soon see that you have got the best part of your father's belongings."

But the cat's master did not build his hopes too high. After all, a cat dressed in boots and carrying a bag is still only a cat. But then he remembered seeing Puss play a great many cunning tricks to catch rats and mice, such as when he used to hang by his heels, or hide himself in the grain and pretend to be dead. So the youngest son decided to give the cat a chance.

The young master sent for the bootmaker and Puss was carefully fitted and measured. Soon the boots arrived and very fine boots they were, too. Puss pulled them on as easily as if he had been wearing them all his life. A smart hat and a stout bag were also found for him and the first thing Puss did was to stuff the bag with bran and thistles. Then he tiptoed into the rabbit warren, stretched

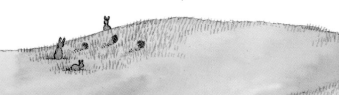

out upon the ground
and, holding the string
of the bag in his paws, he
pretended to be dead.

Now older, more experienced rabbits would not fall for such a trick, but Puss lay quietly and hoped that the younger bunnies might be tempted by the tasty titbits inside his bag.

Soon, after much sniffing and nibbling, he had what he wanted. A rash and foolish young rabbit jumped right into the bag, and Master Puss quickly drew the strings tight! The poor rabbit kicked with all his might but in a trice he was dead. Well pleased, Puss took his sack to the Palace and asked to speak with His Majesty, the King. Puss strode into the throne room, bowed low and said:

"Sir, I have brought you a rabbit — a gift from my noble Lord, the Marquis of Carabas," (for that was the new title which Puss had made up for his Master)

"We hope your Royal
Majesty will enjoy it."

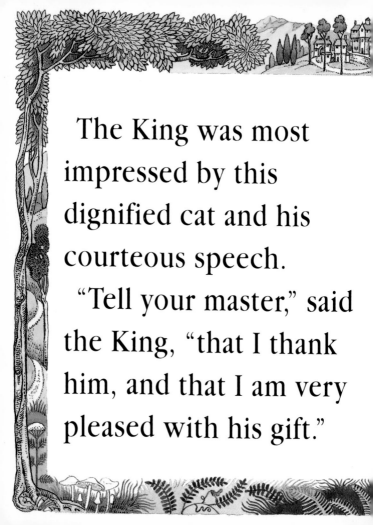

The King was most impressed by this dignified cat and his courteous speech.

"Tell your master," said the King, "that I thank him, and that I am very pleased with his gift."

Some days later, the cat went and hid himself in the corn field, holding his bag open as before. This time a couple of young partridges ran into the bag and Puss quickly drew the strings tight.

Once again the cat visited the Palace and, with a twirl of his whiskers, he presented his catch to the King.-

"From my noble Lord, the Marquis of Carabas," he explained.

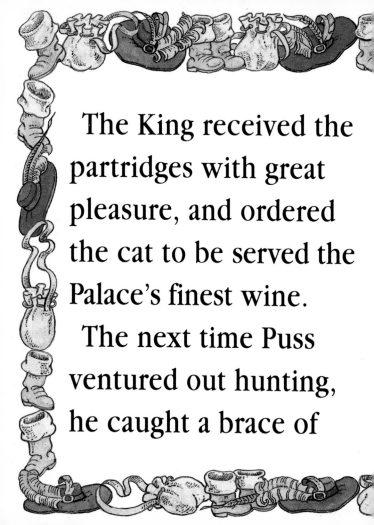

The King received the partridges with great pleasure, and ordered the cat to be served the Palace's finest wine.

The next time Puss ventured out hunting, he caught a brace of

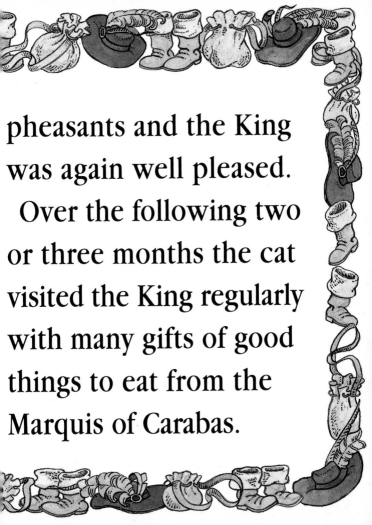

pheasants and the King was again well pleased.

Over the following two or three months the cat visited the King regularly with many gifts of good things to eat from the Marquis of Carabas.

One day Puss heard that the King was preparing to take a drive by the river with his daughter, the beautiful Princess.

The clever cat returned
to his master and said:
"If you do as I tell you
your fortune will be made.
Go and wash yourself in
the river and leave
everything else to me."
Greatly puzzled, the

young man did as he was told. He went down to the river, undressed and waded into the water. While he was washing he heard the clatter of horses' hooves coming closer along the road.

Soon the King passed
by in his coach. At once
the cat began to cry out:

"Help! help! My Lord
Marquis of Carabas is
drowning! Help! Help!"

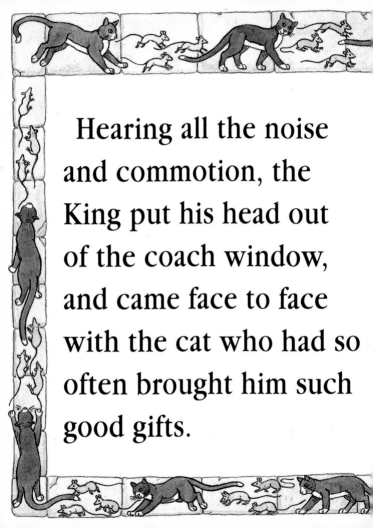

Hearing all the noise and commotion, the King put his head out of the coach window, and came face to face with the cat who had so often brought him such good gifts.

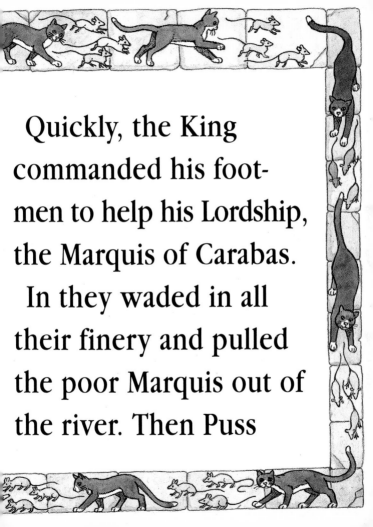

Quickly, the King commanded his foot-men to help his Lordship, the Marquis of Carabas. In they waded in all their finery and pulled the poor Marquis out of the river. Then Puss told the King that while his Master was washing, some rogues had stolen all his clothes

But what the cunning cat had really done was hide the clothes under a great big stone. For he

realised that his young
master could not possibly
meet the King dressed in
such shabby attire.

The King immediately commanded his servants to run to the Palace and fetch a selection of his best suits for the Lord Marquis of Carabas.

When he was dressed in his fine new clothes,

the cat's master made a
most impressive figure.
The Princess secretly
thought him the most
handsome man she had

ever seen, and he was
equally taken with her.

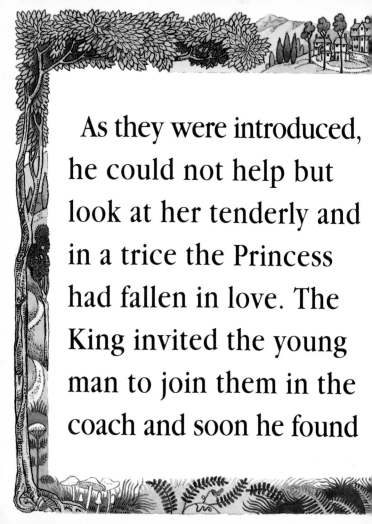

As they were introduced, he could not help but look at her tenderly and in a trice the Princess had fallen in love. The King invited the young man to join them in the coach and soon he found himself sitting next to the Princess. The cat was quite overjoyed to see his plan beginning to succeed. He ran on ahead of the coach and soon came upon some mowers in a meadow,

busy at work with their scythes. Scowling fiercely, the cat spoke to them.

"Good people, the King is heading this way. If you do not tell him that the meadow you mow

belongs to my Lord
Marquis of Carabas, you
shall be chopped as small
as herbs for the pot."

Along came the King
and, asking his coachman
to stop, he leaned out of
the window and spoke
to the mowers.

"Good people," he said. "This is a lush meadow. To whom does this fine field belong?"

"To my Lord Marquis of Carabas," they all replied together, for the cat's threats had made

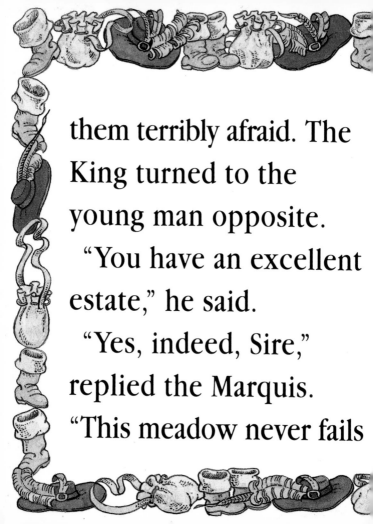

them terribly afraid. The
King turned to the
young man opposite.

"You have an excellent
estate," he said.

"Yes, indeed, Sire,"
replied the Marquis.
"This meadow never fails

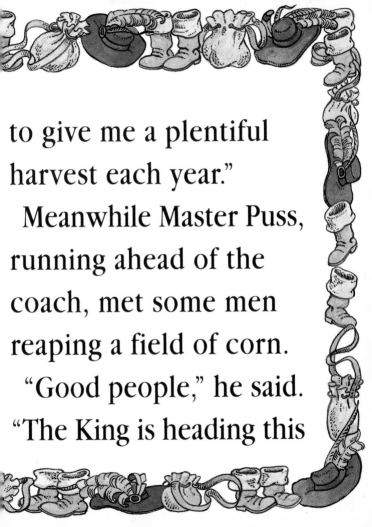

to give me a plentiful
harvest each year."

Meanwhile Master Puss,
running ahead of the
coach, met some men
reaping a field of corn.

"Good people," he said.
"The King is heading this

way. If you do not tell him that all this corn belongs to the Marquis of Carabas, you shall be chopped as small as herbs for the pot."

The King, who passed by a moment later, was indeed curious to know who owned such a splendid field of corn.

"It is my Lord Marquis of Carabas," replied the reapers, and the King was very impressed and again congratulated the Marquis on his fine land.

And so they continued on their way. The cat ran ahead of the coach and warned each and every person he met that they should tell the King the same story. And so they did until the King was quite astonished by the vast estates of the Lord Marquis of Carabas.

"Almost as large as my own," he thought.

Soon Master Puss came to a magnificent castle. Now he had taken great care to discover all he could about the master of this castle. He knew that he was an ogre and, what is more, the richest

ogre in all the land —
and it was he who owned
all the fine estates through
which the King had
been driven.

The cat marched
straight up to the huge
castle and called out:

"Oh, Master Ogre! I could not pass so close to your fine castle without having the honour of paying my respects."

The ogre was flattered by this little speech and, in as polite a manner as

was possible for such a
fierce creature, he
invited Puss inside.

"I have heard," said the
cat, "that you have magic

powers. I have been told that you have the gift of being able to change yourself into any sort of creature you want. Is it true that you can turn yourself into a lion, or an elephant?"

"That is true," answered the ogre proudly, "and if you don't believe me, watch this!"

With a flash and a bang, there stood a huge lion! Opening his jaws wide, the creature let out a fierce roar.

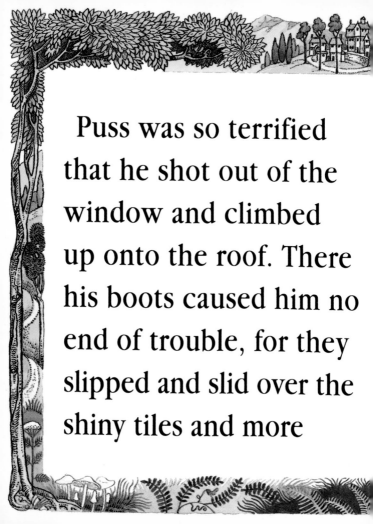

Puss was so terrified that he shot out of the window and climbed up onto the roof. There his boots caused him no end of trouble, for they slipped and slid over the shiny tiles and more than once he nearly fell to his death. From the room below him came the sound of laughing and, feeling a little foolish, the cat climbed down and scrambled in through the window.

"I must admit," he told the ogre, "that I was scared out of my wits by your ferocious lion. I would not have believed such a thing possible had I not seen it with my own eyes."

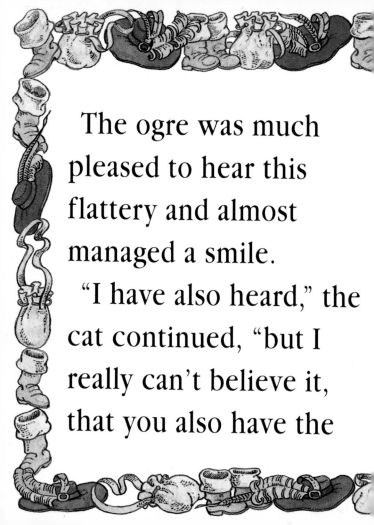

The ogre was much pleased to hear this flattery and almost managed a smile.

"I have also heard," the cat continued, "but I really can't believe it, that you also have the

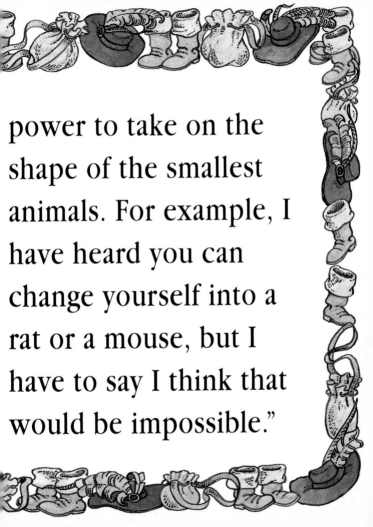

power to take on the
shape of the smallest
animals. For example, I
have heard you can
change yourself into a
rat or a mouse, but I
have to say I think that
would be impossible."

"Impossible?" cried the ogre. "Just watch this!"
And with a flash and a bang he changed himself into a mouse and began to run about the floor.

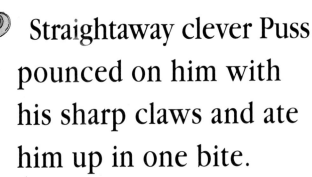

Straightaway clever Puss
pounced on him with
his sharp claws and ate
him up in one bite.

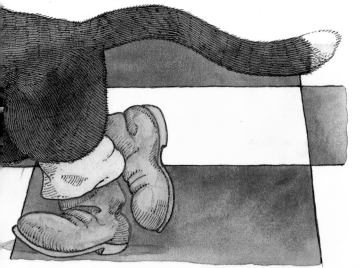

And so, with the ogre gone for good, the cunning Puss succeeded in winning for his master the finest castle in all the land.

Meanwhile the Royal coach was approaching.

The King was curious
to know who lived in
such a splendid place.
When Puss heard the
rumble of his Majesty's
coach crossing the
bridge, he ran out and
bowed before the King.

"Your Majesty is most welcome at this castle, home of my Lord Marquis of Carabas," he said.

"What! My Lord Marquis," cried the King, "so this fine castle also belongs to you! What a beautiful courtyard! What magnificent buildings! I should very much like to take a closer look."

And so the King entered
the castle, followed by
his daughter, who held
the Marquis by the hand.

They walked into a huge hall and there spread before them was a splendid banquet, for the ogre had been expecting visitors that very day and had prepared a special feast. The cat scurried hither and thither as he served the royal guests and the Marquis behaved all the while as if he had always been a noble Lord!

As the meal drew to an end, the King, who had drunk five or six glasses

of the ogre's best wine,
felt very contented. He
had been watching my
Lord Marquis of Carabas

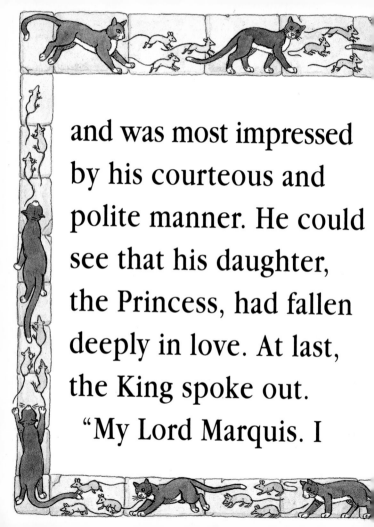

and was most impressed by his courteous and polite manner. He could see that his daughter, the Princess, had fallen deeply in love. At last, the King spoke out.

"My Lord Marquis. I

have been most pleased by all that I have seen today. I would like to offer you the honour of becoming my son-in-law and, if you don't accept, then you will only have yourself to blame."

The Marquis could hardly believe his ears. He looked at the Princess and, blushing with pleasure, she smiled back happily. The clever cat was so pleased that his plan had finally worked

and he had won for his master all the riches and happiness his heart could ever desire, that he scampered out into the courtyard and performed fourteen cartwheels straight off! And so the

Marquis of Carabas and the Princess were married that very same day.

Puss was made a noble Lord, and never again had to chase after mice — well, only when he fancied some fun!

The
Three Little Pigs

Illustrated by Jenny Press

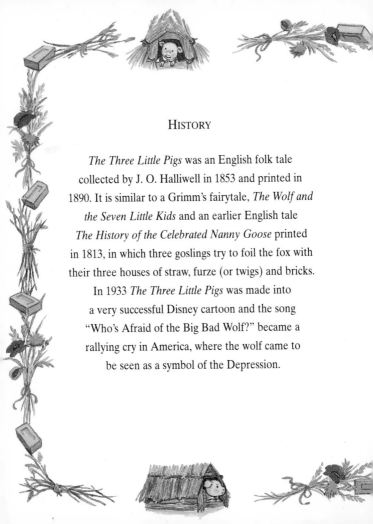

HISTORY

The Three Little Pigs was an English folk tale
collected by J. O. Halliwell in 1853 and printed in
1890. It is similar to a Grimm's fairytale, *The Wolf and
the Seven Little Kids* and an earlier English tale
The History of the Celebrated Nanny Goose printed
in 1813, in which three goslings try to foil the fox with
their three houses of straw, furze (or twigs) and bricks.
In 1933 *The Three Little Pigs* was made into
a very successful Disney cartoon and the song
"Who's Afraid of the Big Bad Wolf?" became a
rallying cry in America, where the wolf came to
be seen as a symbol of the Depression.

Once upon a time there were three little pigs. They lived at home with their mother in a snug little house close by a babbling brook. The three pigs were very

fond of their food, as
most pigs are, and soon
they had grown up to be
big and strong.

Gradually, the snug little house became too small for the three of them.

At meal times they had trouble sitting round the little kitchen table. Most of the time it was a terrible squeeze.

In the bathroom, they had trouble getting their toothbrushes near their teeth. And upstairs in the bedroom, they had trouble getting their trousers over the right trotters!

One day their mother spoke out.

"You are big enough now to find houses of your own," she said. "Take good care of yourselves — and watch out for the big, bad wolf!"

So the three little pigs
set off down the road.

Soon they met a man carrying a large bundle of straw.

"Please may I have some straw to build a house?" asked the first little pig.

"Certainly you may," replied the man.

Straightaway, the pig set to work and in a short while had finished

his very own house, made entirely of straw. It was a little shaky — but very warm and dry.

"The wolf won't catch me now!" declared the first little pig proudly.

The other two little

pigs carried on down
the road. Soon they met
a man carrying a large
bundle of sticks.

"Please may I have some sticks to build a house?" asked the second pig.

"Certainly you may," replied the man. Soon the little pig was hard at work and when he was finished, he stood back

and admired his fine new home. It was a little draughty — but it looked good and strong.

"What a fine house," he said. "The wolf certainly won't catch me now!"

The third little pig

walked on down the
road and soon met a man
carrying a large load of
bricks.

"Please may I have some bricks to build a house?" asked the third little pig.

"Certainly you may," replied the man. All day long the pig worked on his house. He mixed

cement, he built thick walls and as the sun went down, he laid his very last brick.

"Excellent!" he said. "The wolf won't catch me now!"

The very next day who

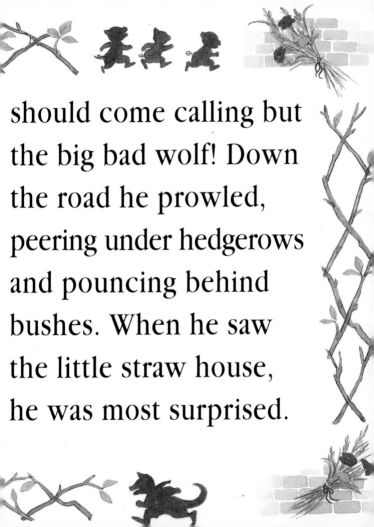

should come calling but the big bad wolf! Down the road he prowled, peering under hedgerows and pouncing behind bushes. When he saw the little straw house, he was most surprised.

"I wonder who lives here?" he said. And he decided to have a look.

He crept up to the
window and quietly
peeked inside.

There was the first
little pig, tucking into a
large plate of porridge.
With a big smile on his
face, the big bad wolf

knocked gleefully at the
front door.

"Little pig, little pig,
let me come in," called
the wolf in a growly
voice. The first little pig
dropped his spoon in
fright.

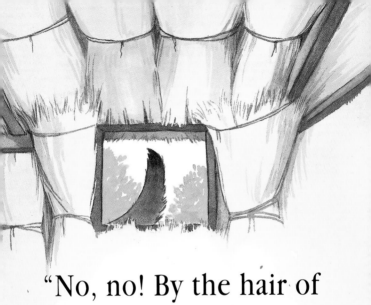

"No, no! By the hair of my chinny chin chin, I will NOT let you in!" he shouted.

"Then I'll puff, and I'll huff, and I'll blow your house in!" shouted the

wolf. The poor little pig
trembled and stuffed his
trotters in his ears.

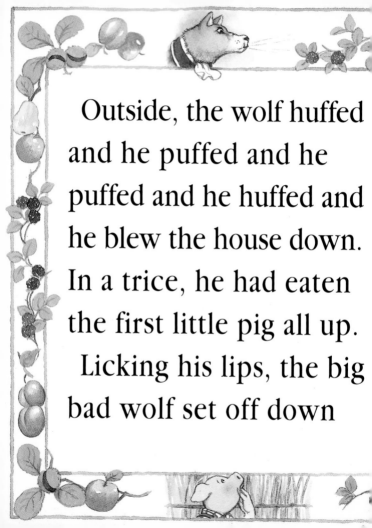

Outside, the wolf huffed and he puffed and he puffed and he huffed and he blew the house down. In a trice, he had eaten the first little pig all up. Licking his lips, the big bad wolf set off down

the road. Soon he saw a
nice little house made
all of sticks.

"I wonder who lives
here?" said the wolf. He
tiptoed up to the
window and peeped
inside. There was the

second little pig, just
finishing his third cup
of tea.

   With a wicked grin,
the big bad wolf marched
up and knocked loudly
at the front door. Rat,
tat, tat! he went.

"Little pig, little pig, let me come in," he called. The second little pig jumped in the air, spilling hot tea all over his toast.

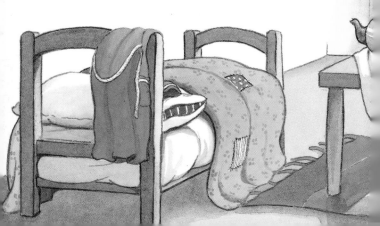

"No, no! By the hair on my chinny chin chin, I will NOT let you in!" he shouted.

"Then I'll huff and I'll puff, and I'll blow your house in!" shouted the wolf. The little pig hid under the table. Outside, the wolf laughed. Then he huffed and he puffed and he puffed and he huffed and he blew the house down. In two ticks, he had eaten the second little pig all up.

Patting his stomach, the big bad wolf strolled on down the road. Soon he came upon a smart house made of bricks.

"I wonder who lives in this fine house?" cried the wolf with a wink and a sly smirk. Inside, the third little pig sat back in his comfortable armchair and carried on reading his newspaper.

He wasn't at all bothered by that silly old wolf.

"Little pig, little pig," the wolf called softly through the letterbox. "Little pig, little pig. Let me come in."

The little pig shook his newspaper crossly.

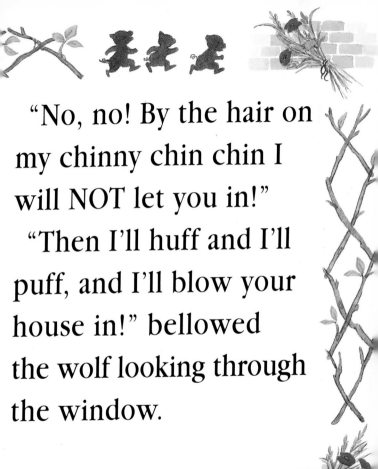

"No, no! By the hair on my chinny chin chin I will NOT let you in!"

"Then I'll huff and I'll puff, and I'll blow your house in!" bellowed the wolf looking through the window.

"Puff away! Huff away!"
replied the pig carelessly.
"You don't scare me!"

The wolf just smiled. He had blown down the house of straw. He had blown down the house of sticks. He was sure he could blow down a house of bricks.

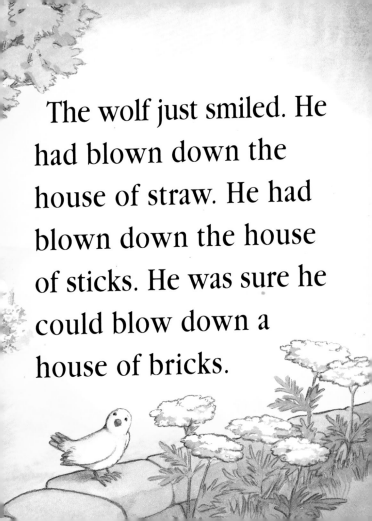

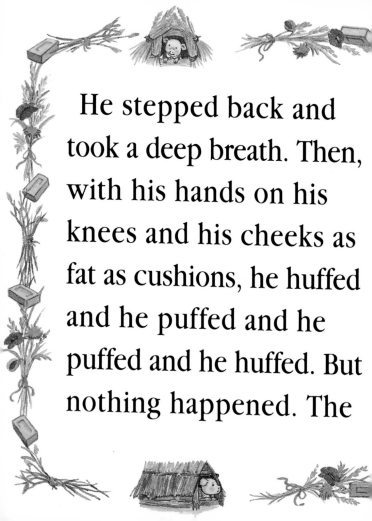

He stepped back and took a deep breath. Then, with his hands on his knees and his cheeks as fat as cushions, he huffed and he puffed and he puffed and he huffed. But nothing happened. The

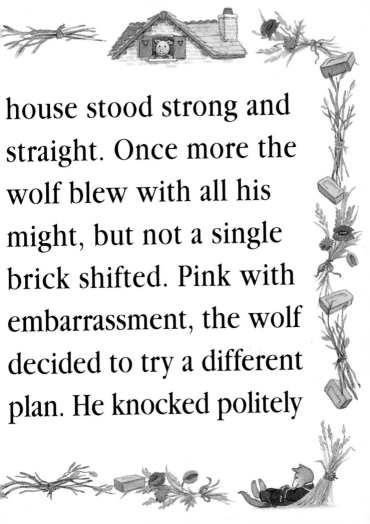

house stood strong and straight. Once more the wolf blew with all his might, but not a single brick shifted. Pink with embarrassment, the wolf decided to try a different plan. He knocked politely on the little pig's door.

"Oh, little pig, I hear you like turnips. Well, the best turnips grow in Father Smith's field and if you can be ready at six o'clock in the morning I will take you there."

"I'll be ready," replied the little pig.

So the next morning at six o'clock the wolf came calling at the door.

"Are you ready, little pig?" he cried.

"Ready?" replied the pig.

"I was ready long ago. I have already fetched my turnips and now they are cooking in my pot!"

The wolf turned red with anger. He could smell a delicious aroma wafting from the little

pig's chimney. Slowly
the wolf counted to ten
and tried to calm himself.
He had another plan.

"Oh, little pig. I know you like apples. Well, tomorrow morning at five o'clock I am going to Merrygarden Farm to pick as many as I like. If you can be ready you can come with me."

"I'll be ready," replied the little pig.

The next morning the little pig left his house at four o'clock to be sure to beat the wolf — but he wasn't quick enough! He was high up an apple tree, eating his fill, when the big bad wolf arrived.

"Ah, there you are," called the wolf. "Are the apples good?" The pig nearly fell out of the tree in fright. The wolf had him trapped! How he wished he was safe at home inside his strong house of bricks. Slowly the wolf prowled around the trunk, never taking his eyes off the pig for a second. Then the little pig had a clever idea.

"Those really are very tasty apples, Mr. Wolf,"

he called down. "Surely
you would like to try
one?"

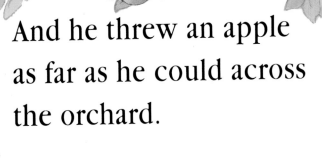

And he threw an apple
as far as he could across
the orchard.

The greedy wolf went bounding after it and, in a flash, the pig was down the tree and running for home, licketty-spit.

The wolf turned purple with rage, but was determined not to be

beaten by the clever
little pig. He called at
the house the next day.

"I am going to the fair
this afternoon. Would
you like to come with
me?" he asked, in as
friendly a voice as he

could manage. The little
pig looked out through
his letterbox.

"Another trick!" thought the little pig. "Well, I got to the turnips before him. I got to the apples before him. I'm sure I will be able to get to the fair before him," and so the little pig agreed to meet the wolf at three o'clock. But at two o'clock the pig set off on his own. He had a lovely time at the fair and bought a beautiful big butter churn. On his way home he spied the wolf

coming up the hill towards him. The little pig was much afraid.

"Trapped again!" he cried. "What shall I do?" He clasped his barrel to his chest and frantically looked around for

somewhere to hide. But the fields stretched out on all sides without so much as a thorn bush or a holly hedge to give him cover. Then the pig looked at his butter churn and laughed.

"This will save me," he chuckled and into the barrel he jumped. It rolled down the road, faster and faster.

It frightened the wolf
so much that he nearly
leapt out of his skin!

The pig rolled on down
the road and soon was
safe and sound at home.
He was just tucking
into his second slice of

apple cake when there was a timid knock at the door.

The pig looked through the window and there stood the wolf, with knees knocking, looking very worried indeed.

"A horrible monster
attacked me on the way
to the fair," he quavered.
The pig thought this
was very funny.

"Why, that was me in my butter churn," he laughed.

When the wolf heard this, he nearly exploded.

"Little pig, little pig," he shouted. "I am going to climb down your chimney and eat you all up right now!"

Quickly the pig lit a fire under his large pot of water. As the flames leapt higher and higher, the water bubbled hotter and hotter.

The wolf climbed up to the roof. He made a terrible noise, slipping on the brick tiles.

The little pig listened hard and heard the wolf reach the chimney pot.

Clatter, clatter! went the wolf's claws and soon the little pig could hear him squeezing his way down the chimney.

When the little pig saw the end of the wolf's tail, he lifted the lid of his cooking pot. Down came the wolf and with a splash! he fell straight into the boiling water.

Clang! Back went the lid

and soon the wolf was dead.

But, as I expect you can guess, the third little pig lived happily ever after and was never troubled by a big bad wolf again!

Goldilocks
and the
Three Bears

Illustrated by Nigel McMullen

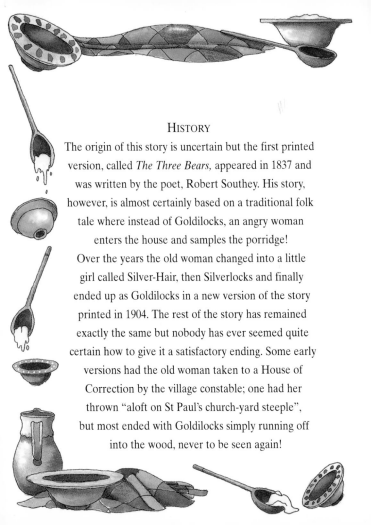

History

The origin of this story is uncertain but the first printed version, called *The Three Bears,* appeared in 1837 and was written by the poet, Robert Southey. His story, however, is almost certainly based on a traditional folk tale where instead of Goldilocks, an angry woman enters the house and samples the porridge!

Over the years the old woman changed into a little girl called Silver-Hair, then Silverlocks and finally ended up as Goldilocks in a new version of the story printed in 1904. The rest of the story has remained exactly the same but nobody has ever seemed quite certain how to give it a satisfactory ending. Some early versions had the old woman taken to a House of Correction by the village constable; one had her thrown "aloft on St Paul's church-yard steeple", but most ended with Goldilocks simply running off into the wood, never to be seen again!

Once upon a time there were Three Bears. There was a large, gruff Father Bear, a middle-sized Mother Bear and a little, small, wee Baby Bear.

Father Bear wore baggy
checked trousers held up
with old blue braces.

His tweed jacket had leather patches on the elbows and was a little too tight around the tummy. He loved his food and never left the house without a small snack wrapped up in a red

spotted handkerchief
which he tucked away
inside his cloth cap.

"Just to fill the corners,"
he explained, patting
his round furry stomach.

Mother Bear was plump
and cuddly. She had

dimples in her chubby cheeks and she winked her eyes whenever she laughed, which was often because she was a very jolly bear. She wore a blue and white spotted dress with a deep frill.

She smelled of currant buns and warm bread, especially on baking day. Then she would cook tray after tray of good things to eat, until

the kitchen table could
hold no more and her
face was dotted with
white smudges of flour.

Baby Bear was the sweetest little bear you could ever imagine. His golden fur was as soft as thistledown. His shining brown eyes were full of mischief and his little button nose was as black

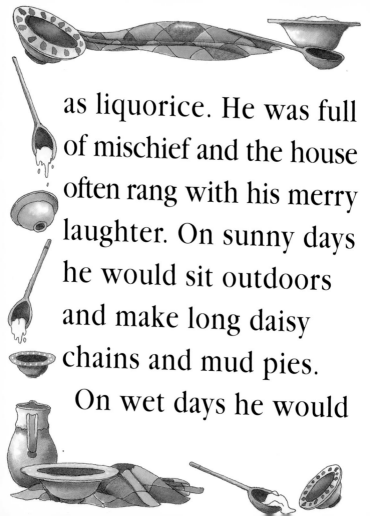

as liquorice. He was full
of mischief and the house
often rang with his merry
laughter. On sunny days
he would sit outdoors
and make long daisy
chains and mud pies.

On wet days he would

snuggle on his mother's lap and watch the raindrops run races down the windowpanes.

The Three Bears lived all together in a little wooden house right in the middle of a forest.

The house was as warm
and as snug as a dormouse
nest. Father Bear was a
very clever carpenter
and had made all the

furniture himself. There
was a fine carved table
and a cupboard for
their bear essentials.

Tucked around the table were three fine chairs. There was a large chair for Father

Bear, a middle-sized chair for Mother Bear and a little, small, wee chair for Baby Bear.

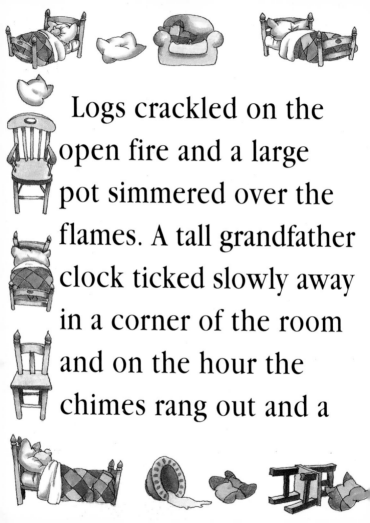

Logs crackled on the open fire and a large pot simmered over the flames. A tall grandfather clock ticked slowly away in a corner of the room and on the hour the chimes rang out and a

little hatch would open
at the top of the casing.
Out bobbed a brown
honey bee on a bouncing
spring, followed by
three little bears: a
Father Bear, a Mother
Bear and a Baby Bear.

The bears hopped and danced as they chased the bee with outstretched paws — but they never quite caught up and, as the chimes ended, the bee always flew back into the clock ahead of them.

Upstairs were three beds and a wardrobe for their bear necessities. There was a great big bed for Father Bear, a middle-sized bed for Mother Bear and a little, small, wee bed for Baby Bear.

Mother Bear had stitched patchwork quilts for each of the beds and cushions to pile high on the chairs.

Baby Bear had painted bright pictures which they hung on the walls.

Outside in the garden honey bees buzzed round the hives and doves cooed in the dovecot. A scarebearcrow stood guard over the vegetables and tall sunflowers nodded by the gate.

The Three Bears loved their little home and thought the forest was a wonderful place to live. In the spring, the trees were bursting with new buds. Joyful birdsong was carried on the warm

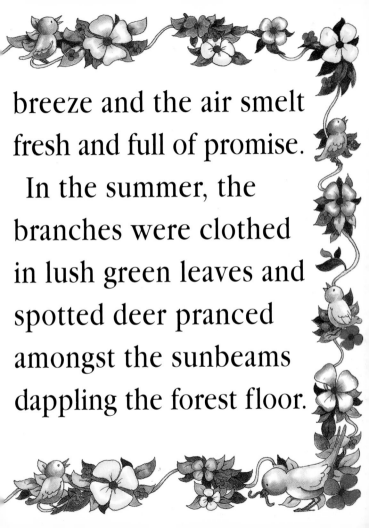

breeze and the air smelt fresh and full of promise.

In the summer, the branches were clothed in lush green leaves and spotted deer pranced amongst the sunbeams dappling the forest floor.

When autumn came the leaves fell — yellow, orange, gold and brown. They gathered in deep drifts and Baby Bear loved to kick through them as he walked through the wood.

In the winter, the bare branches stood stark against a grey sky. Icicles dripped from the eaves of the little house and all the forest sounds were muffled under a deep blanket of snow.

Every morning —
spring, summer, autumn
and winter — the Three
Bears had porridge for
their breakfast.

"It builds you big and
strong!" boomed Father
Bear, as he sat down.

"It warms up your tummy!" smiled Mother Bear, as she tucked in.

"And it tastes yummy!" giggled Baby Bear.

There was a large porridge bowl for Father Bear, a middle-

sized porridge bowl for
Mother Bear and a little,
small, wee porridge
bowl for Baby Bear.

Father Bear's bowl was red with white spots. Mother Bear's bowl was green and painted with yellow marigolds. Baby Bear's bowl was blue and had brown honey pots all around the rim.

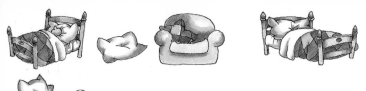

One sunny morning
the Three Bears all sat
down together to have
their breakfast but they
found the porridge was
much too hot to eat.

"Let's go for a walk in
the forest while our

porridge cools down,"
said Father Bear.

Now, while they were
out walking, who
should come by but a
little girl. She had long
golden hair and her
name was Goldilocks.

"What a sweet little house," said Goldilocks. "I wonder if anyone is at home?"

She looked through the window and peeped through the keyhole but there was no-one to be seen. Goldilocks was a curious little girl so she lifted the door latch and stepped inside.

"Hello," she called. "Is there anybody there?" But all was quiet and still. Then Goldilocks saw the porridge on the table. "Mmmm, that looks good!" she said, licking her lips. Now if Miss

Goldilocks was a polite little girl she would have waited until the Bears came home. Then, perhaps, they would have invited her to share their breakfast, for they were good Bears.

They were a little rough sometimes, as Bears can be, but for all that very gentle and friendly.

But Goldilocks was a naughty little girl and did not want to wait.

First, she tasted Father Bear's porridge, but that was too hot. Then she tasted Mother Bear's porridge, but that was

too cold. So then she
picked up Baby Bear's
tiny spoon and tasted
his porridge. It wasn't
too hot and it wasn't
too cold. It was just right!
In next to no time Baby
Bear's bowl was empty.

Greedy Goldilocks had eaten it all up!

Now she felt so full of porridge that she had to sit down. First she tried Father Bear's chair. It had a flat wooden seat and a high back made of thin wooden spindles. Goldilocks sat down — but she soon scrambled off again.

"What a horrid, hard chair!" she complained. Then she tried Mother Bear's chair. It was large and squishy and filled to overflowing with fat feather cushions.

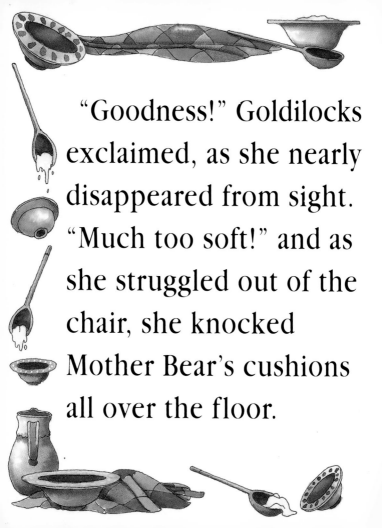

"Goodness!" Goldilocks exclaimed, as she nearly disappeared from sight. "Much too soft!" and as she struggled out of the chair, she knocked Mother Bear's cushions all over the floor.

Then she tried Baby
Bear's little rocking
chair. Father Bear had
carved garden flowers
into the oak and hidden
amongst them were all
the birds of the forest.
Goldilocks sat down.

It wasn't too hard and it wasn't too soft. This chair was just right! "Perfect!" sighed Goldilocks, happily.

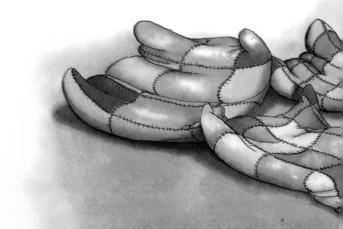

With a tummy full of porridge and a big smile on her face, Goldilocks leant back and made herself comfortable. But she was too big and heavy for Baby Bear's little chair and with a

creak and a crash, it
broke into tiny pieces.
  Goldilocks was cross!
"Maybe I can rest
upstairs," she thought
and up the rickety
wooden stairs she went.
  The bedroom was tucked

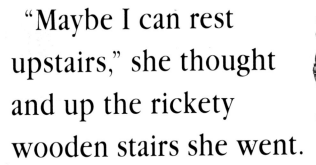

under the rafters in the
roof. It was cosy and
warm and Goldilocks
yawned sleepily as she

looked at the three beds.
First she tried to lie
down on Father Bear's
big bed, but it was so

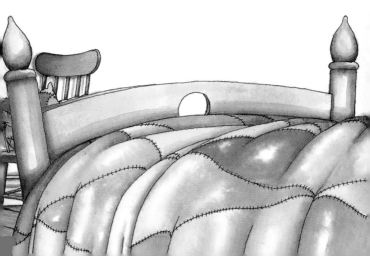

high that she could not climb up onto it. She tried to pull herself up but only succeeded in pulling the pillow onto the floor!

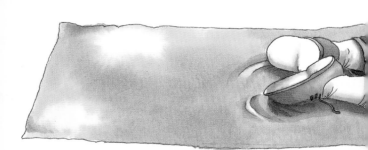

"I can't climb up there," she sighed. Then she sat down on Mother Bear's bed. It was soft and squidgy and very, very low down.

"It will feel as if I am sleeping on the floor and I won't like that," complained Goldilocks.

Then she spotted Baby
Bear's little bed. It wasn't
too high and it wasn't
too low. It was just right!

So Goldilocks climbed
into Baby Bear's bed,
pulled the eiderdown
up to her chin and was
soon fast asleep.

Shortly after, the Three
Bears arrived back home
from their walk. They

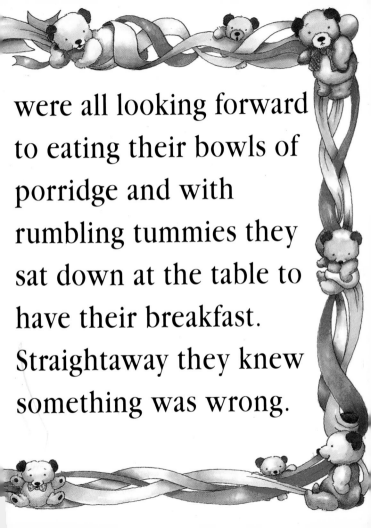

were all looking forward to eating their bowls of porridge and with rumbling tummies they sat down at the table to have their breakfast. Straightaway they knew something was wrong.

"Someone's been eating my porridge!" roared Father Bear.

Mother Bear looked at her plate.

"Someone's been eating my porridge!" she growled.

Then the little, small, wee Baby Bear looked at his empty plate.

"Someone's been eating my porridge," he squeaked, "and they've eaten it all up!"

The Three Bears looked around them. Then Father Bear noticed that his favourite seat had been moved from its usual position close by the fireside.

"Someone's been sitting

in my chair!" Father
Bear bellowed.

Mother Bear saw that
her soft cushions were
lying all over the floor.

"Someone's been sitting
in my chair!" she grunted.

Then Baby Bear realised

that the wooden splinters covering the rug were all that remained of his favourite little chair. "Someone's been sitting in my chair," he wailed, "and they've broken it into pieces!"

Then the Three Bears
decided to hunt all
through the house until
they found the naughty
person who had visited
them whilst they were
out walking in the forest.
Up the rickety wooden

stairs they all went,
thump! thump! thump!
Straightaway, Father
Bear noticed that the
pillow had been pulled
off his bed.

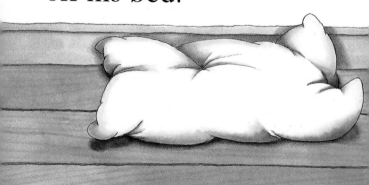

"Someone's been sleeping in my bed!" he grumbled.

Then Mother Bear looked closely at her bed and saw that her blanket was crumpled. "Someone's been

sleeping in my bed!"
she rumbled.

And when Baby Bear
came to look at his bed,
who should he find
tucked up under the
covers but a little girl
with long golden hair!

"Someone's been sleeping in my bed," he squealed, "and she's still there!"

Now Baby Bear's voice was so squeaky and shrill that it woke up Goldilocks at once. And what a fright she had when she saw the Three Bears looking so fierce and cross!

Up she jumped and ran like the wind down the rickety wooden stairs.

Out of the door she flew and she didn't stop running until she was far away from the little house and the Three

Bears. And, after that, they never saw Goldilocks again!

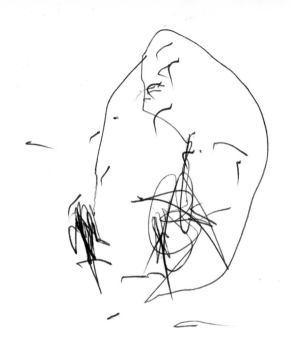